'I cou[ld] [see] she w[as] terribly afraid, but I didn't soften anything; instead, seeing that she was afraid I deliberately intensified it.'

FYODOR DOSTOYEVSKY
Born 1821, Moscow, Russia
Died 1881, Saint Petersburg, Russia

The story was first published in its original Russian as 'Krotkaya' in 1876 and is taken from the *The Gambler and Other Stories*.

DOSTOYEVSKY IN PENGUIN CLASSICS
Crime and Punishment
Anna Karenina
The Idiot
The Double
The Gambler and Other Stories
The Grand Inquisitor
Notes from the Underground
Netochka Nezvanova
The House of the Dead
The Brothers Karamazov
The Village of Stepanchikovo
Russian Short Stories from Pushkin to Buida
Demons
Poor Folk and Other Stories

FYODOR DOSTOYEVSKY

The Meek One

A Fantastic Story

Translated by
Ronald Meyer

PENGUIN BOOKS

PENGUIN CLASSICS

Published by the Penguin Group
Penguin Books Ltd, 80 Strand, London WC2R ORL, England
Penguin Group (USA) Inc., 375 Hudson Street, New York, New York 10014, USA
Penguin Group (Canada), 90 Eglinton Avenue East, Suite 700, Toronto, Ontario,
Canada M4P 2Y3 (a division of Pearson Penguin Canada Inc.)
Penguin Ireland, 25 St Stephen's Green, Dublin 2, Ireland
(a division of Penguin Books Ltd)
Penguin Group (Australia), 707 Collins Street, Melbourne, Victoria 3008, Australia
(a division of Pearson Australia Group Pty Ltd)
Penguin Books India Pvt Ltd, 11 Community Centre, Panchsheel Park,
New Delhi – 110 017, India
Penguin Group (NZ), 67 Apollo Drive, Rosedale, Auckland 0632, New Zealand
(a division of Pearson New Zealand Ltd)
Penguin Books (South Africa) (Pty) Ltd, Block D, Rosebank Office Park,
181 Jan Smuts Avenue, Parktown North, Gauteng 2193, South Africa

Penguin Books Ltd, Registered Offices: 80 Strand, London WC2R ORL, England

www.penguin.com

This edition published in Penguin Classics 2015
002

Translation copyright © Ronald Mayer, 2010

The moral right of the translator has been asserted

Set in 9/12.4 pt Baskerville 10 Pro
Typeset by Jouve (UK), Milton Keynes
Printed in Great Britain by Clays Ltd, St Ives plc

A CIP catalogue record for this book is available from the British Library

ISBN: 978-0-141-39748-1

www.greenpenguin.co.uk

Penguin Books is committed to a sustainable
future for our business, our readers and our planet.
This book is made from Forest Stewardship
Council™ certified paper.

Chapter 1

I. WHO I WAS AND WHO SHE WAS

... Now as long as she's here – everything is still all right: I'm constantly going over and looking at her; but tomorrow they'll take her away and – how will I ever stay behind all on my own? Now she's on the table in the sitting room, on two card tables that were put together, and the coffin will come tomorrow, a white one, with white *gros de Naples*, however, that's not it ... I keep pacing and want to make sense of it for myself. Now it's six hours that I've been trying to make sense of it and I still can't collect my thoughts to a T. The fact of the matter is that I keep pacing, pacing, pacing ... Here's how it was. I'll simply tell it in order. (Order!) Gentlemen, I'm far from being a literary man, as you'll see, well, so be it, but I'll tell it as I myself understand it. That's the horror of it for me, that I understand everything!

If you want to know, that is, if we take it from the very beginning, then quite simply she used to come to me to pawn things in order to pay for advertising in the *Voice*, saying, well, that there's a governess, willing to travel and give lessons in the home and so forth and so on. That was in the very beginning and of course I didn't single her out from the others: she came like all the others and so forth. But afterwards I began to single her out. She was so thin, fair, a bit taller than average; with me she was always awkward, as if she were embarrassed (I think that she was exactly the

1

same with all strangers, and, it goes without saying, I was no different than anyone else, that is, if taken not as a pawn-broker but as a man). As soon as she received her money she would immediately turn around and leave. And all in silence. Others argue, beg, haggle to be given more; but not this one, whatever she was given . . . It seems to me that I keep getting muddled . . . Yes; first of all, I was struck by her things: silver gilt earrings, a worthless little locket – things worth twenty kopecks. She herself knew that they were worth all of ten kopecks, but I could see from her face that for her they were objects of great value – and indeed, as I learned later, this was all that she had left from her papa and mama. Only once did I permit myself to smile at her things. That is, you see, I never permit myself that, I maintain a gentlemanly tone with the public: a few words said respectfully and sternly. 'Sternly, sternly and sternly.' But she suddenly permitted herself to bring the remnants (quite literally, that is) of an old rabbit-skin jacket – and I couldn't resist and suddenly said something to her in the way of a witticism, as it were. Goodness gracious, how she flared up! Her eyes were blue, large, thoughtful, but how they blazed! But she didn't let drop a single word, she picked up her 'remnants' and left. That was the first time that I noticed her *particularly* and thought something of that sort about her, that is, precisely something of that particular sort. Yes; I recall yet another impression, that is, if you wish, the main impression, the synthesis of everything: namely, that she was terribly young, so young, as if she were fourteen years old. Whereas she was then three months shy of sixteen. However, that wasn't what I wanted to say, that wasn't the synthesis at all. She came

again the next day. I later learned that she had been to
Dobronravov and Mozer with that jacket, but they don't take
anything except gold and didn't even bother to talk to her.
I, on the other hand, had once taken a cameo from her
(a worthless little thing) – and when I gave it some thought
later on I was surprised: I also don't buy anything except
gold and silver and yet I had taken a cameo. That was my
second thought about her then, I remember that.

This time, that is, after going to Mozer, she brought an
amber cigar holder – a so-so little piece, for the connoisseur,
but something of no worth to us, because we deal only in
gold. Since she had come after yesterday's *rebellion*, I greeted
her sternly. Sternness for me means dryness. However, as I
was giving her the two roubles, I couldn't resist and said
with some irritation, as it were: 'I'm doing this only *for you*,
Mozer wouldn't take a thing like this from you.' I particularly emphasized the words 'for you', and precisely with a
certain insinuation. I was angry. Once again she flared up,
upon hearing that 'for you', but she held her tongue, didn't
throw down the money, took it – that's what poverty is! But
how she flared up! I understood that I had wounded her.
But when she had gone, I suddenly asked myself: So is this
triumph over her really worth two roubles? Hee-hee-hee! I
remember that I asked precisely that very question twice: 'Is
it worth it? Is it worth it?' And, laughing, I answered this
question to myself in the affirmative. Then I really cheered
up. But this wasn't a nasty feeling: I had a plan, a purpose;
I wanted to test her, because suddenly I began to have some
thoughts about her. That was my third *particular* thought
about her.

... Well, it was from that time that it all started. It goes without saying, I immediately tried to find out all her circumstances indirectly and waited for her arrival with particular impatience. You see, I had a feeling that she would come soon. When she came, I launched into an amiable conversation with unusual politeness. You see, I wasn't badly brought up and have manners. Hmm. That was when I guessed that she was kind and meek. The kind and meek don't resist for long, and although they are by no means very open, they don't at all know how to avoid a conversation: they answer grudgingly, but they answer and the longer it goes on, the more they answer; but if this is what you want, you can't let yourself get tired. It goes without saying that she didn't explain anything to me then. It was later that I learned about the *Voice* and about everything else. She was then mustering every last bit she had to advertise – at first, it goes without saying, presumptuously: 'Governess, willing to travel, send terms by post'; but later: 'Willing to do anything, tutor, be a companion, housekeeping, care for the sick, can sew' and so forth and so on. The usual! It goes without saying that all this was added to the advertisement at different stages, and towards the end, when despair had set it, there was even 'without salary, for board'. No, she didn't find a position! I made up my mind then to test her for the last time: I suddenly picked up today's *Voice* and showed her an advertisement: 'Young female, orphan, seeks position as governess of small children, preferably with an elderly widower. Willing to do light housework.'

'There, you see, this was published this morning and by

evening she's sure to have found a job. That's the way to advertise!'

Again she flared up, again her eyes blazed; she turned around and immediately walked out. I was very pleased. However, by then I was already sure of everything and had no fears: nobody would take her cigar holders. Besides, she had already run out of cigar holders. And so it was, two days later she comes, such a pale, agitated little thing – I understood that something had happened at home, and indeed something had happened. I'll explain straight away what happened, but now I merely wish to recall how I suddenly did something chic and rose in her eyes. A plan suddenly occurred to me. The fact of the matter is that she brought this icon (she had steeled herself to bring it) . . . Oh, listen! Listen! This is where it began, but I keep getting muddled . . . The fact of the matter is that I now want to recall everything, every trifle, every little detail. I still want to collect my thoughts to a T and – I can't, and now there are these little details, these little details . . .

An icon of the Mother of God. The Mother of God with Child, a family heirloom, an antique, with a silver gilt frame – worth – well, worth about six roubles. I see that the icon is dear to her, and she's pawning the whole icon, without removing the mounting. I tell her that it would be better if she removed the mounting and took the icon with her, because after all it's an icon.

'Surely you're not forbidden?'

'No, it's not that it's forbidden, but just that, perhaps, you yourself . . .'

'Well, remove it.'

'You know what, I won't remove it, but I'll put it over there in the icon case,' I said, after giving it some thought, 'with the other icons, under the lamp.' (I've always had the lamp burning ever since I opened my shop.) 'And I'll give you ten roubles – it's as simple as that.'

'I don't need ten, give me five; I'll redeem it without fail.'

'But don't you want ten? The icon is worth it,' I added, after observing that her little eyes had flashed once again. She held her tongue. I brought her five roubles.

'Don't despise anybody – I've been in tight squeezes myself, and even a bit worse, and if you now see me in such an occupation . . . well, you see, after all that I've endured . . .'

'You're taking revenge on society? Is that it?' she suddenly interrupted me with a rather sarcastic gibe, in which, however, there was a good deal of innocence (that is, of a general sort, because she certainly did not single me out from the others then, so it was said almost inoffensively). 'Aha!' I thought, 'so that's what you're like, your character is showing itself, you belong to the new movement.'

'You see,' I immediately observed, half-jokingly, half-mysteriously. 'I – I am part of that part of the whole that desires to do evil, but creates good . . .'

She looked at me quickly and with great curiosity, in which, however, there was a great deal of childishness:

'Wait a moment . . . What's that saying? Where's it from? I've heard it somewhere . . .'

'Don't rack your brains: Mephistopheles recommends himself to Faust in those words. Have you read *Faust?*'

'No . . . not carefully.'

'That is, you haven't read it at all. You should read it. However, once again I see a sardonic grin on your lips. Please, don't suppose that I have so little taste that I wished to paint over my role as a pawnbroker by recommending myself to you as Mephistopheles. Once a pawnbroker, always a pawnbroker. We know that, miss.'

'You're such a strange person . . . I didn't in the least want to say anything of the kind . . .'

She wanted to say: I didn't expect that you were an educated man, but she didn't say it, though I knew that she had thought it; I had pleased her terribly much.

'You see,' I observed, 'one can do good in any walk of life. Of course, I'm not speaking of myself; let's suppose that I do nothing but bad things . . .'

'Of course, one can do good in any position,' she said, looking at me with a quick and penetrating glance. 'Precisely in any position,' she added suddenly.

Oh, I remember, I remember all those moments! And I also want to add that when these young people, these dear young people, want to say something intelligent and penetrating, then their faces suddenly show you all too sincerely and naively: 'Here I am, I'm telling you something intelligent and penetrating.' And it's not at all from vanity, as is the case with the likes of us, but you see that she herself sets great store on all this terribly, and she believes, and respects and thinks that you, too, respect all this just as she does. Oh, sincerity! That's what they win you over with! And it was so charming in her!

I remember, I have forgotten nothing! When she left, I made up my mind at once. That same day I made my final enquiries and learned absolutely everything else there was to know about her present particulars; all the particulars of her past I already knew from Lukerya, who was then their servant and whom I had bribed several days earlier. These circumstances were so horrible that I don't understand how it had been possible for her to laugh, as she had that day, and be curious about Mephistopheles' words, when she herself was faced with such horrors. But – youth! That's precisely what I thought about her then with pride and joy, because, you see, there was also magnanimity about it, as if she were to say: the great works of Goethe shine even on the brink of ruin. Youth is always magnanimous, if only ever so slightly and ever so distortedly. That is, I'm speaking of her, you see, her alone. And the main thing, I then looked upon her as *mine* and did not doubt my power. You know, that's a most voluptuous thought, when you no longer have any doubt.

But what's wrong with me? If I keep going on like this, then when will I collect everything to a T? Quickly, quickly – this isn't the point at all, oh God!

II. A MARRIAGE PROPOSAL

The 'particulars' I learned about her I can set forth in a few words: her father and mother had died a long time ago, three years previously, and she had been left with her disreputable aunts. That is, it's saying too little to call them disreputable. One aunt was a widow with a large family, six children, each one smaller than the next; the other was a spinster, old and nasty. Both of them were nasty. Her father had been a government official, but only a clerk, and a non-hereditary nobleman – in a word: everything played into my hands. I appeared as if from some higher world: after all, I was a retired staff captain of a brilliant regiment, a nobleman by birth, independent and so on, and as far as the pawnshop went, the aunts could only look at it with respect. She had been slaving for her aunts for three years, but nevertheless she had passed an examination somewhere – she had managed to pass it, snatched a free minute to pass it, despite relentless work day in and day out – and that meant something about aspirations for the noble and the sublime on her part. After all, why did I want to get married? But who cares about me, we'll save that for later . . . As if that were the point! She taught her aunt's children, she sewed their underclothes, and towards the end she washed not only these underclothes, but she, with her bad chest, also washed the floors. To put it bluntly, they even beat her, reproaching her for every crumb. It ended with them intending to sell her. Ugh! I'll omit the dirty details. Later she told me everything in detail. A neighbour, a fat shopkeeper, had been observing all this for a whole year, and he wasn't just an ordinary shopkeeper, but the owner of two grocery stores. He had already beat two wives to death and was looking for a third, and had cast his eye on her: 'She's a quiet one,' he thought, 'she grew up in poverty and I'm marrying for the sake of my orphans.' Indeed, he did have orphans. He began to seek her hand, started negotiations with the aunts, and on top of that – he's fifty years old; she's horrified. And that's when she started coming to me to get money for advertisements in the *Voice*.

In the end, she began asking the aunts to give her just the littlest bit of time to think it over. They gave her that little bit, but only one, they didn't give her another; they badgered her: 'We don't know where we'll get our next meal, even without an extra mouth to feed.' I already knew all this, and on that same day, after her visit in the morning, I made up my mind. That evening the merchant came, he had brought from the shop a pound of candies worth fifty kopecks; she's sitting with him, and I summon Lukerya from the kitchen and tell her to go to her and whisper that I'm standing by the gate and wish to tell her something most urgently. I remained pleased with myself. And in general I was terribly pleased with myself that entire day.

Right there at the gate, already dumbfounded that I had summoned her, I explained to her, in Lukerya's presence, that I would consider myself happy and honoured . . . Secondly, she was not surprised by my manner or by the fact that this was taking place by the gate: 'I am a straightforward man,' I said, 'and have studied the circumstances of the matter.' And I wasn't lying that I'm straightforward. Well, to hell with it. I spoke not only decently, that is, by showing myself to be a person of good breeding, but originally as well, and that's the main thing. What, is it a sin to acknowledge this? I want to judge myself and am doing so. I must speak both *pro* and *contra*, and I am doing so. I recalled it with delight afterwards, even though it was stupid: I announced straight out then, without any embarrassment, that, in the first place, I wasn't particularly talented, not particularly intelligent, and perhaps not even particularly kind, that I was a rather cheap egoist (I remember this expression, I had composed it on my way there and remained pleased with it) and that – very, very likely – there was much that was unpleasant about me in other respects as well. All this was said with a particular kind of pride – we know how these sorts of things are said. Of course, I had sufficient good taste, after nobly declaring my deficiencies, not to launch into a declaration of my virtues: 'But to make up for this, I have this, that and the other.' I could see that she was still terribly afraid, but I didn't soften anything; instead, seeing that she was afraid I deliberately intensified it: I said straight out that she wouldn't go hungry, but as for fancy clothes, the theatre and balls – there would be none of that, though perhaps later, when I had achieved my goal. I was definitely carried away by this stern tone. I added, and as casually as possible, that if I had taken up such an occupation, that is, keeping this pawnshop, it was for one purpose only – that is, there was a certain circumstance, so to speak . . . But you see I had a right to speak like that: I really did have such a purpose and such a circumstance. Wait a moment, gentlemen, all my life I have been the first to hate this pawnbroking business, but in essence, you see, even though it's ridiculous to talk to oneself in mysterious phrases, I was 'taking revenge on society', you see, I really, really, really was! Therefore, her joke about the fact that I was 'taking revenge' was unfair. That is, you see, if I had said to her straight out in so many words: 'Yes, I'm taking revenge on society', and she had burst out laughing, the way she did that morning, it would indeed have come out ridiculous. But with an indirect hint and by dropping a mysterious phrase it turned out that it was possible to engage her imagination. Moreover, I wasn't afraid

11

of anything then: you see, I knew that in any event the fat shopkeeper was more repulsive than I and that I, standing by the gate, was her liberator. I understood that, you see. Oh, man understands baseness particularly well! But was it baseness? How is one to judge a man in a case like this? Didn't I love her already even then?

Wait a moment: it goes without saying that I didn't say a word to her about doing a good deed: on the contrary, oh, on the contrary: 'It is *I*,' I said, 'who am being done the favour, and not *you*.' So that I even expressed this in words, I couldn't help myself, and perhaps it came out stupidly, because I noticed a fleeting grin on her face. But on the whole I had definitely won. Wait a moment, if I'm going to recall all this filth, then I'll recall this final bit of swinishness: I was standing there and this is what was going through my head: You're tall, fit, educated and – and finally, to speak without any boasting, you're not bad looking. That's what was running through my head. It goes without saying, she said 'yes' there and then by the gate. But . . . but I should add: she thought it over for a long time, right there and then by the gate, before she said 'yes'. She was so deep in thought, so deep in thought that I was on the verge of asking, 'Well, what is it going to be?' – and I couldn't even help myself from asking with a certain sense of chic: 'Well, what is it going to be, Miss?' – adding the 'Miss' for good measure.

'Wait, I'm thinking.'

And her little face was so serious, so serious – that even then I might have read it! But instead I was offended: 'Is she really,' I thought to myself, 'choosing between me and the merchant?' Oh, I still didn't understand then! I still didn't understand anything, anything then! I didn't understand until today! I remember Lukerya ran after me when I was already walking away, stopped me in the street and said, catching her breath: 'God will reward you, sir, for taking our dear young lady – only don't say anything about it to her, she's proud.'

Well now, proud! I like them proud, I said to myself. The proud ones are particularly nice, when . . . well, when you no longer harbour any doubts about your power over them. Eh? Oh, base, awkward man! Oh, how pleased I was! Do you know, while she was standing there by the gate deep in thought about whether to say 'yes' to me, and I was surprised, do you know, that she might even have been thinking: 'If it's to be misfortune either way, isn't it better to choose the worst straight away, that is, the fat shopkeeper; let him get drunk, the sooner the better, and beat me to death!' Eh? What do you think, could that have been what she was thinking?

And even now I don't understand, even now I don't understand anything! I just now said that she might have been thinking that she should choose the worse of the two misfortunes, that is, the merchant. But who was worse for her then – the merchant or I? The merchant or the pawnbroker who quotes Goethe? That's still a question! What question? You don't understand even that: the answer is lying on the table, and you say 'what question'! But to hell with me! I'm not the point here at all . . . And at the same time, what do I care now – whether I'm the point or not? That's something I'm utterly incapable of deciding. I'd better go to bed. I have a headache . . .

III. THE NOBLEST OF MEN,
BUT I DON'T BELIEVE IT MYSELF

I didn't fall asleep. And how could I with that pulse hammering away in my head. I want to absorb all this, all this filth. Oh, the filth! Oh, the filth I dragged her out of then! She should have realized that, you know, she should have appreciated my deed! I was pleased, too, by various thoughts, for example, that I was forty-one years old and that she was only sixteen. That fascinated me, this sense of inequality, it was very sweet, very sweet.

I, for example, wanted to have the wedding *à l'anglaise*, that is, just the two of us, perhaps with two witnesses, one of whom would be Lukerya, and then at once to the train, for example, if only to Moscow (it so happened that I had business there), to a hotel for a fortnight or so. She was against it, she wouldn't have it and I was forced to visit her aunts and pay my respects to them as the relatives from whom I was taking her. I gave in, and the aunts were rendered their due. I even made a present of a hundred roubles each to those creatures and promised more, of course, without saying a word to her, so as not to distress her with the baseness of the situation. The aunts at once became as soft as silk. There was an argument about the trousseau as well: she didn't have anything, almost literally, but she didn't want anything either. However, I managed to convince her that it wasn't possible to have absolutely nothing, and so I arranged for the trousseau myself, because who else would do anything for her? Well, but to hell with me! Various ideas of mine, however, I nevertheless did manage to convey to her then, so that she would at least know. Perhaps I was even too hasty. The main thing is that from the very beginning, however much she tried to hold out, she would throw herself at me with her love; she would meet me when I came home in the evening with rapture, she would tell me in her prattle (the charming prattle of innocence!) all about her child-hood, youth, about her parental home, about her father and mother. But I immediately threw cold water on all these ecstasies right then and there. That was the whole point of my idea. I answered her raptures with silence, gracious, of course . . . but she nevertheless quickly saw that we were different and that I was – a riddle. And the main thing is that I had set my sights on this riddle! You see, it was in order to pose this riddle perhaps that I committed all this foolishness! First of all, sternness – it was with sternness that I took her into my house. In a word, even though I was quite pleased with things as they were, I began to create a complete system. Oh, it took shape on its own, without any effort. And it couldn't have been otherwise, I had to create this system on account of one incontrovertible circumstance – really, what is this? I'm slandering myself! The system was genuine. No, listen, if you're going to judge a person, then you should judge him knowing the case . . . Listen.

How should I begin this, because it's very difficult. When you begin justifying yourself – that's when it gets difficult. You see: young people despise money, for example – I ham-mered away about money; I pressed home about money. And I hammered away so that she began to fall silent more and more. She would open her big eyes, listen, look and fall silent. You see: young people are magnanimous, that is, the good ones are magnanimous and impetuous, but they have little tolerance, as soon as something's not quite right – you get their contempt. But I wanted breadth, I wanted to instil breadth right into her heart, to instil it into her heart's vista, isn't that so? I'll take a trivial example: How could I explain, for example, my pawnshop to a person like that? It goes without saying that I didn't bring it up directly, or it would have looked like I was asking her forgiveness for the pawnshop; instead I acted, so to speak, with pride – I spoke almost silently. And I'm a master of speaking silently – all my life I've spoken silently and I've lived through entire tragedies in silence. Oh, and I too have been unhappy! I was cast aside by everyone, cast aside and forgotten, and no one, no one knows it! And suddenly this sixteen-year-old girl got hold of details about me afterwards from vile people and thought that she knew everything, but meanwhile the secret remained only in this man's breast! I went on being silent, and I was particularly, particularly silent with her until just yesterday – why was I silent? Because I'm a proud man. I wanted her to find out on her own, without me, but not from stories told by scoundrels, but that she should *guess herself* about this man and comprehend him! When I received her into my house, I wanted her complete respect. I wanted her to stand before me beseechingly, on account of my suffering – and I was worthy of that. Oh, I've always been proud, I've always wanted all or nothing! And that's precisely why I'm not for half-measures in happiness, but wanted everything – and that's precisely why I was forced to act as I did then, as if to say: 'Figure it out for yourself and appreciate me!' Because, you must agree, if I had begun by explaining and prompting, being evasive and asking for respect – then, you see, it would have been as if I were asking for charity ... However ... However, why am I talking about this!

Stupid, stupid, stupid, stupid! I straight away and ruthlessly (and I want to emphasize that it was ruthlessly) explained to her then, in a few words, that the magnanimity of young people was lovely, but not worth a brass button. Why not? Because it comes cheap, they get it without having lived; it's all, so to speak, the 'first impressions of existence', but let's see you do some work! Cheap magnanimity is always easy, and even to give your life – even that's easy, because that's just a matter of the blood boiling and an over-abundance of energy, one passionately longs for beauty! No, take an act of magnanimity that is difficult, quiet, muted, without splendour, where you're slandered, where there's much sacrifice and not a drop of glory – where you, a shining man, are brought forward before everyone as a scoundrel, when you are the most honest man in the world – come on, try your hand at that sort of deed, no, sir, you'll give it up! While I – all I've done my whole life is to shoulder that sort of deed. In the beginning she would argue – and how! But then she began to fall silent, completely and totally, she would just open her eyes terribly wide as she listened, such big, big eyes, and so attentive. And ... and besides that I suddenly saw a smile, a mistrustful, silent, bad smile. It was with that smile that I brought her into my house. And it's also true that she had nowhere else to go ...

17

IV. PLANS AND MORE PLANS

Which of us was the first to begin then?

Neither. It began on its own from the very first. I have said that I had brought her into my house with sternness; however, I softened it from the very first. When she was still my fiancée it had been explained to her that she would assist in taking in the pledges and paying out the money, and she didn't say anything then (note that). And what's more, she even took to the business with zeal. Well, of course, the apartment, the furniture – everything remained the same as before. The apartment has two rooms: one is a large room in which the shop is partitioned off from the rest, and the other one is also a large room in which we have our sitting room and bedroom. My furniture isn't much; even her aunts had better. My icon-stand with the lamp is in the room with the shop; in the other room I have my bookcase with some books and a trunk to which I have the keys; and there's a bed, tables, chairs. When she was still my fiancée I told her that one rouble a day and no more was allotted for our board, that is, food, for me, her and Lukerya, whom I had enticed away: 'I need 30,000 in three years,' I told her, 'otherwise I won't be able to save up enough money.' She didn't stand in the way, but I myself added to our board by thirty kopecks. It was the same thing with the theatre. When she was still my fiancée I told her that there wouldn't be any theatre; however, I decided that we should go to the theatre once a month, and decently at that, in the orchestra. We went

together, three times, and saw *In Pursuit of Happiness* and
Songbirds, I think. (Oh, to hell with it, to hell with it!) We
went in silence and returned in silence. Why, why did
we from the very beginning choose to be silent? After all,
there weren't any quarrels in the beginning, but there was
silence then, too. As I recall, she somehow kept looking at
me then on the sly; when I noticed that I increased my
silence. True, I was the one who insisted upon silence, and
not she. On her part there were outbursts once or twice,
when she would rush to embrace me; but since these outbursts were unhealthy and hysterical, and what I required
was steadfast happiness, together with her respect, I received
them coldly. And I was right to do so: each time the outburst
was followed the next day by a quarrel.

That is, there weren't any quarrels, but there was silence
and – and on her part a more and more insolent look. 'Rebellion and independence' – that's what it was, only she didn't
know how. Yes, that meek face was becoming more and more
insolent. Can you believe it? I was becoming repulsive to
her – I came to understand that. And there could be no
doubt about these outbursts that came over her. For example,
after leaving behind such filth and beggary, after scrubbing
floors, how could she suddenly begin to grumble about our
poverty! You see, gentlemen: it wasn't poverty, it was econ-
omy, and where necessary there was some luxury, when it
came to linens and cleanliness, for example. I had always
dreamed before that cleanliness in a husband attracts a wife.
However, it wasn't poverty, but my supposed miserly econ-
omy that bothered her: 'He has goals, he's showing his firm

character.' She suddenly declined to go to the theatre. And there was more and more of that sardonic grin . . . While I intensified my silence, I intensified my silence.

Surely there was no need to justify my actions? The main thing here was the pawnshop. Come now, sirs: I knew that a woman, especially one who was sixteen years old, couldn't help but submit completely to a man. Women have no originality, that's – that's an axiom, even now it's an axiom for me! Never mind what's lying there in the front room: truth is truth, and even Mill himself can't do anything about it! But a loving woman, oh, a loving woman idolizes even the vices, even the villainy of her beloved being. He would not seek such justifications for his villainy as she will find for him. That's magnanimous but not original. It is this lack of originality alone that has been the undoing of women. And what, I repeat, what are you pointing to there on the table? Is there really anything original about what's there on the table? Oh-h-h!

Listen: I was certain of her love then. You see, she would throw herself on my neck then. That meant she loved me, or rather – she wished to love me. Yes, that's what it was: she wished to love, she sought to love. But the main thing, you see, is that there weren't any villainies for which she needed to find justifications. You say a 'pawnbroker' and that's what everyone says. But what if I am a pawnbroker? That means there are reasons, if the most magnanimous of men became a pawnbroker. You see, gentlemen, there are ideas . . . that is, you see, when some ideas are said out loud, put into words, they come out terribly stupid. They come out so that you're ashamed of them yourself. But why? For no reason at all. Because we're all good-for-nothings and can't bear the truth, or I don't know why else. I said just now 'the most magnanimous of men'. That's ridiculous, you see, and yet that's how it was. You see, it's the truth, that is, it's the most truthful truth of all! Yes, I *had the right* then to want to provide for myself and open this shop: 'You, that is, you people, have spurned me, you have driven me away with your contemptuous silence. You have answered my outbursts of passion with an insult that I will feel for the rest of my life. Consequently, I now am within my rights to protect myself from you with a wall, to amass those 30,000 roubles and end my days somewhere in the Crimea, on the southern shore, amidst mountains and vineyards, on my own estate purchased with that 30,000, and the main thing, far away from you all, but without malice towards you, with an ideal in my soul, with my beloved woman at my heart, with a family if God should send one, and – helping out the neighbouring peasants.' It goes without saying that it's good that I'm telling this to myself now, but what could have been more stupid than if I had described all this out loud to her then? That was the reason behind my proud silence, and that was the reason we sat in silence. Because what would she have understood? Just sixteen years old, so very young – what could she have understood of my justifications, of my suffering? I was dealing with straightforwardness, ignorance of life, cheap, youthful convictions, the blindness of 'beautiful hearts', and the main thing, the pawnshop and – *basta*! (But was I a scoundrel in the pawnshop, didn't she see how I conducted myself and did I charge more than I should?) Oh, how terrible is truth on this earth! This charming one, this meek one, this heaven – she was a tyrant, the unbearable tyrant of my soul and my tormentor! I'd be slandering myself, you see, if I didn't say that! You think I didn't love her? Who can say that I didn't love her? You see: there was irony here, the malicious irony of fate and nature! We are accursed, the life of people in general is accursed! (And mine in particular!) I understand now, you see, that I made some mistake here! Something didn't come out the way it was supposed to. Everything was clear, my plan was as clear as the sky: 'Severe, proud, requires no moral consolation, suffers in silence.' That's how it was, I wasn't lying, I wasn't lying! 'She'll see for herself later on that there was magnanimity here, but she just wasn't able to see it now – and when she does fathom it some day, she'll appreciate it ten times more and will fall down in the dust with her hands folded in supplication.' That was the plan. But I forgot something here or failed to take it into account. I wasn't able to do something here. But enough, enough. And of whom can I ask forgiveness now? What's done is done. Take courage, man, and be proud! It's not you who are to blame! . . .

Now then, I'll tell the truth, I won't be afraid to stand face to face with the truth: *she* is to blame, *she* is to blame! . . .

V. THE MEEK ONE REBELS

The quarrels began when she suddenly took it into her head to pay out money as she saw fit, to appraise things for more than they were worth, and a couple of times she even thought fit to enter into an argument with me on the subject. I didn't agree. But then this captain's widow turned up.

An old lady, the widow of a captain, came with a locket – a present from her late husband, well, you know, a keepsake. I gave thirty roubles. She started to whine plaintively, begging me to keep the thing for her; it goes without saying that we keep it. Well, in a word, suddenly she comes five days later to exchange it for a bracelet that's not worth even eight roubles; it goes without saying that I refused. She must have guessed then something from my wife's eyes, but in any case she came when I wasn't there, and my wife exchanged the locket.

When I learned about it that very same day, I began by speaking meekly, but firmly and reasonably. She was sitting on the bed, looking at the floor, tapping the rug with the toe of her right shoe (her gesture); an unpleasant smile played on her lips. Then without raising my voice at all I announced calmly that the money was *mine*, that I had the right to look at life with *my own* eyes and that when I invited her into my house I had not concealed anything from her.

She suddenly jumped up, suddenly began trembling all over and – what do you think – she suddenly began stamping her feet at me; this was a wild animal, this was a fit, this was a wild animal having a fit. I froze in astonishment: I had never expected such an outburst. But I didn't become flustered, I didn't even move a muscle, and once again in the same calm voice I declared plainly that from that time forward I refused to let her take part in my affairs. She laughed in my face and walked out of the apartment.

The fact of the matter is that she had no right to leave the apartment. Nowhere without me, that was the agreement we made when she was still my fiancée. She returned towards evening; I didn't say a word.

The next day, too, she went out in the morning, and it was the same thing the following day. I locked up the shop and set off to see her aunts. I had broken off relations with them from the day of the wedding – I hadn't invited them to visit me, we didn't visit them. Now it turned out that she wasn't with them. They heard me out with curiosity and laughed in my face. 'Serves you right,' they said. But I had expected their laughter. I then and there bribed the younger aunt, the spinster, with a hundred roubles, and gave her twenty-five in advance. Two days later she comes to me: 'An officer,' she says, 'a Lieutenant Yefimovich, a former comrade of yours from the regiment, is mixed up in this.' I was quite aston-ished. This Yefimovich had done me more harm than anyone else in the regiment, and a month ago he stopped by my shop a couple of times, and being the shameless fellow that he is, under the pretence of pawning something, I remember, he began laughing with my wife. I went up to him then and told him that, considering our relations, he should not pre-sume to visit me; but no idea of anything like that crossed my mind, I simply thought that he was an insolent fellow. But now suddenly her auntie informs me that she had made an appointment to see him and that this whole affair is being handled by a certain former acquaintance of the aunts, Yuliya Samsonovna, a widow, and a colonel's widow at that – 'It's her that your spouse goes to visit now,' she says.

I'll cut this story short. This business cost me almost 300 roubles, but in two days it was arranged that I would stand in the adjoining room, behind closed doors, and listen to my wife's first *rendezvous* alone with Yefimovich. Meanwhile, the previous evening a brief but for me very significant scene between myself and my wife took place.

She returned towards evening, sat down on the bed, looked at me mockingly and thumped the rug with her foot. Suddenly, as I was looking at her, the idea flew into my head then that all this past month, or, rather, for the past two weeks, she had not been herself at all – one could even say that she had been exactly the opposite: a wild, aggressive being had made its appearance; I can't say shameless, but disorderly and looking for trouble. Asking for trouble. Meekness, however, held her back. When a girl like that starts creating an uproar, even if she does cross the line, it's nevertheless plain to see that she's only hurting herself, that she's egging herself on and that she will be the first who is unable to cope with her feelings of modesty and shame. That's why girls like that sometimes go too far, so that you don't believe your own eyes when you witness it. A soul accustomed to debauchery, on the contrary, always softens it, making it more vile, but in a guise of decorum and decency that claims to be superior to you.

'And is it true that you were driven out of your regiment, because you were too cowardly to fight a duel?' she asked suddenly, out of the blue, and her eyes flashed.

'It's true; the officers rendered the verdict that I was to be asked to leave the regiment, although I had in any case already tendered my resignation.'

'You were driven out as a coward?'

'Yes, they judged me a coward. But I refused to duel not

because I was a coward, but because I didn't wish to submit to their tyrannical verdict and issue a challenge to a duel when I did not consider myself to be insulted. You should know,' I couldn't restrain myself here, 'that flying in the face of such tyranny through my actions and accepting all the consequences took far more courage than any duel would have done.'

I couldn't contain myself, with this phrase I launched into self-justifications, as it were, and that was all she needed, a fresh instance of my humiliation. She burst out in malicious laughter.

'And is it true that for the next three years you wandered the streets of Petersburg like a tramp, and begged for kopecks, and slept under billiard tables?'

'I even spent some nights in the Vyazemsky House on Haymarket Square. Yes, it's true; in my life after leaving the regiment there was much shame and degradation, but not moral degradation, because I was the first to loathe my actions even then. It was merely the degradation of my will and mind, and it was brought about only by the desperation of my situation. But this passed . . .'

'Oh, now you're an important person – a financier!'

That is, a hint at my pawnshop. But I had already managed to hold myself in check. I saw that she thirsted for explanations that would be humiliating for me and – I didn't give them. Fortunately, a client rang the bell just then and I went to see him in the front room. Afterwards, an hour later, when she had suddenly dressed to go out, she stopped in front of me and said:

'You didn't tell me anything about this before the wedding, however.'

I didn't answer, and she left.

And so, the next day I stood in this room behind the door and listened to my fate being decided, and in my pocket there was a revolver. She was dressed up, sitting at the table, and Yefimovich was putting on airs. And what do you know: it turned out (I say this to my credit), it turned out exactly as I had foreseen and supposed, though without realizing that I had foreseen and supposed this. I don't know whether I'm expressing myself clearly.

This is what happened. I listened for a whole hour and for that hour I witnessed a duel between the most noble and lofty woman and a worldly, depraved, dim-witted creature with a grovelling soul. And how, I thought to myself in amazement, how does this naive, this meek, this reserved girl know all this? The cleverest author of a high-society comedy could not have created this scene of ridicule, the most naive laughter and the holy contempt of virtue for vice. And such brilliance in her words and little turns of speech; what wit in her quick replies, what truth in her censure! And at the same time what almost girlish ingenuousness. She laughed in his face at his declarations of love, at his gestures, at his proposals. Coming straight to the matter with a crude assault and not foreseeing any opposition, all of a sudden he had the wind taken out of his sails. At first I might have thought that it was simply coquetry on her part – the 'coquetry of a clever though depraved creature in order to show herself more lavishly'. But no, the truth shone through like the sun and it was impossible to have any doubts. It was only out of hatred for me, affected and impetuous though it was, that she, inexperienced as she was, could have decided to undertake this meeting, but as soon as it had become reality – her eyes were opened at once. Here was a creature who was simply flailing about so as to insult me no matter what, but once she had decided on such filth she couldn't bear the disorder. And could she, blameless and pure, with ideals, have been attracted to Yefimovich or any of those other high-society brutes? On the contrary, he aroused only laughter. The whole truth rose up from her soul, and indignation called forth sarcasm from her heart. I repeat, towards the end this fool was utterly dazed and sat scowling, barely responding, so that I even began to fear that he would venture to insult her out of mean-spirited revenge. And I repeat once again: to my credit I heard this scene out almost without astonishment. It was as though I had encountered something familiar. It was as though I had gone in order to encounter it. I had gone, believing nothing, no accusation, although I did put a revolver in my pocket – that's the truth! And could I have really imagined her otherwise? Wasn't that why I loved her, wasn't that why I cherished her, wasn't that why I had married her? Oh, of course, I was all too convinced that she hated me then, but I was also convinced of her purity. I brought the scene swiftly to a close by opening the door. Yefimovich jumped to his feet, I took her by the hand and invited her to leave with me. Yefimovich found his bearings and suddenly burst out in resounding peals of laughter.

'Oh, I have no objections to sacred conjugal rights, take

her away, take her away! And you know,' he shouted after me, 'even though a respectable person can't fight you, yet out of respect for your lady, I am at your service . . . If you, however, want to risk it . . .'

'Do you hear that!' I stopped her for a second on the threshold.

Then not a word all the way home. I led her by the hand, and she didn't resist. On the contrary, she was utterly dumb-founded, but only until we got home. On our arrival, she sat down on a chair and fastened her gaze on me. She was extraordinarily pale; though her lips had at once formed a mocking smile, she was already regarding me with a solemn and severe challenge, and, I believe, she was seriously con-vinced those first few moments that I was going to kill her with the revolver. But I took the revolver out of my pocket in silence and laid it on the table. She looked at me and at the revolver. (Note: she was already familiar with this revolver. I had acquired it and kept it loaded ever since open-ing the shop. When I was getting ready to open the shop I had decided not to keep hulking dogs or a burly lackey like Mozer did, for example. The cook opens the door for my visitors. But people who engage in my trade cannot deprive themselves of self-defence, just in case, and I kept a loaded revolver. During those first days when she had come to live in my house she showed a lot of interest in this revolver, she asked a lot of questions, and I even explained the mechanism and how it worked; moreover, I persuaded her once to shoot at a target. Note all that.) Paying no notice of her frightened look, I lay down on the bed half-undressed. I was very tired; it was already almost eleven o'clock. She went on sitting in the same place, without moving, for almost another hour, then she put out the candle and lay down, also dressed, on the sofa by the wall. It was the first time that she didn't come to bed with me – note that as well . . .

VI. A TERRIBLE MEMORY

Now, this terrible memory . . .

I woke up in the morning, between seven and eight, I think, and it was already almost completely light in the room. I woke up all at once fully conscious and suddenly opened my eyes. She was standing by the table, holding the revolver. She didn't see that I was awake and watching. And suddenly I saw that she had started to move towards me, holding the revolver. I quickly shut my eyes and pretended to be fast asleep.

She came up to the bed and stood over me. I heard everything; although a dead silence had fallen, I heard even that silence. Then there came a convulsive movement – and I suddenly, uncontrollably, opened my eyes against my will. She was looking me right in the eyes, and the revolver was already by my temple. Our eyes met. But we looked at each other for no more than a moment. I forced myself to shut my eyes again and at the same moment I resolved with every fibre of my being that I would not stir or open my eyes, no matter what awaited me.

In fact, it does happen sometimes that a person who is sound asleep suddenly opens his eyes, even raises his head for a second and looks about the room, then, a moment later, he lays his head on the pillow again and falls asleep without remembering a thing. When, after meeting her gaze and feeling the revolver at my temple, I suddenly shut my eyes again and didn't stir, like someone sound asleep, she certainly could have supposed that I indeed was asleep and that I hadn't seen anything, particularly since it was altogether incredible that having seen what I saw I would shut my eyes again at *such* a moment.

Yes, incredible. But she still might have guessed the truth – that was what suddenly flashed through my mind, at that very same moment. Oh, what a whirlwind of thoughts, sensations raced through my mind in less than a moment; long live the electricity of human thought! In that case (I felt), if she had guessed the truth and knew that I wasn't sleeping, then I had already crushed her with my readiness to accept death and her hand might now falter. Her former resolve might be shattered by this new extraordinary impression. They say that people standing on a height are drawn downwards, as it were, of their own accord, to the abyss. I think that a lot of suicides and murders have been committed merely because the revolver was already in hand. There's an abyss here as well, there's a forty-five-degree slope down which you can't help but slide and something relentlessly challenges you to pull the trigger. But the awareness that I had seen everything, that I knew everything and that I was awaiting my death from her in silence – might hold her back from that slope.

The silence continued, and suddenly I felt on my temple, at my hairline, the cold touch of iron. You will ask: did I firmly hope that I would be saved? I will answer you as if

I were before God himself: I had no hope whatsoever, except perhaps one chance in a hundred. Why, then, did I accept death? But I will ask: What need would I have of life after the revolver was raised against me by the being whom I adored? Moreover, I knew with all the force of my being that a struggle was going on between us at that very moment, a terrible duel for life and death, a duel of that same coward of yesterday, driven out by his comrades. I knew it, and she knew it, if only she had guessed the truth that I wasn't sleeping.

Perhaps it wasn't like that, perhaps I didn't think that then, but still it must have been like that, even without thought, because all I've done since is think about it every hour of my life.

But you'll ask me the question again: why didn't I save her then from this treachery? Oh, I have asked myself that question a thousand times since – each time when, with a shiver down my spine, I recalled that second. But my soul then was plunged in dark despair: I was lost, I myself was lost, so whom could I have saved? And how do you know whether I still wanted to save somebody then? How can you know what I might have been feeling then?

My consciousness, however, was seething; the seconds passed, there was dead silence; she was still standing over me – and then suddenly I shuddered with hope! I quickly opened my eyes. She was no longer in the room. I got up from the bed: I had defeated her – and she was forever defeated!

I went out to the samovar. We always had the samovar brought to the outer room and she was always the one to pour the tea. I sat down at the table in silence and took a glass of tea from her. About five minutes later I glanced at her. She was terribly pale, even paler than yesterday, and she was looking at me. And suddenly – and suddenly, seeing that I was looking at her, she gave a pale smile with her pale lips, a timid question in her eyes. 'That means that she still has doubts and is asking herself: does he know or not, did he see or didn't he?' I indifferently turned my eyes away. After tea I locked up the shop, went to the market and bought an iron bed and a screen. When I returned home, I had the bed installed in the front room with the screen around it. This bed was for her, but I didn't say a word to her. Even without words she understood from this bed alone that I 'had seen everything and knew everything' and that there was no longer any doubt about this. I left the revolver on the table for the night as always. At night she silently got into her new bed: the marriage was dissolved, 'she had been defeated but not forgiven'. During the night she became delirious, and by morning she had a fever. She was confined to bed for six weeks.

Chapter 2

I. A DREAM OF PRIDE

Lukerya just announced that she won't stay with me and that she'll leave as soon as the mistress is buried. I prayed on my knees for five minutes, and I had wanted to pray for an hour, but I keep thinking, and thinking, and they're all such aching thoughts and my head aches – what's the use of praying – it's nothing but a sin! It's also strange that I don't want to sleep: in great, in such great sorrow, after the first violent outbursts, one always wants to sleep. They say that people who are condemned to death sleep extremely soundly on their last night. As they should, it's only natural, otherwise they wouldn't have the strength to endure it . . . I lay down on the sofa, but I didn't fall asleep . . .

. . . For the six weeks of her illness we took care of her day and night – Lukerya and I and a trained nurse from the hospital, whom I had hired. I didn't begrudge the money, and even wanted to spend money on her. I called in Dr Schroeder and paid him ten roubles a visit. When she regained consciousness, I started to show myself less often. But why am I describing this? When she was completely on her feet again, she sat quietly and silently in my room at a special table, which I had also bought for her at the time . . . Yes, it's true, we were perfectly silent; that is, we began to talk later on, but only about the usual things. Of course, I deliberately refrained from becoming expansive, but I could see very well that she also was happy not to say a word more than was necessary. This seemed perfectly natural on her part: 'She is too shaken and too defeated,' I thought, 'and of course she needs time to forget and get used to things.' And so it was that we were silent, but every minute I was secretly preparing myself for the future. I thought that she was doing the same as well, and it was terribly entertaining for me to guess: Exactly what is she thinking about now?

I'll say one more thing: Oh, of course, nobody knows what

I endured as I grieved over her during her illness. But I kept my grief to myself and kept the grieving in my heart even from Lukerya. I couldn't imagine, I couldn't even suppose that she would die without learning everything. When she was out of danger and her health started to return, I remember this, I quickly calmed down and very much so. What's more, I decided *to postpone our future* for as long as possible, and for the present to leave everything as it was now. Yes, then something happened to me that was strange and peculiar, I don't know what else to call it: I had triumphed and this thought alone proved to be quite sufficient for me. And that's how the whole winter passed. Oh, I was pleased as I had never been before, and that for the whole winter.

You see: in my life there had been one terrible external circumstance, which until then, that is, until the catastrophe with my wife, weighed heavily on me every day and every hour, namely, the loss of my reputation and leaving the regiment. To put it in a nutshell: this had been a tyrannical injustice against me. True, my comrades disliked me on account of my difficult and, perhaps, ridiculous character, although it often happens that what you find sublime, what you hold dear and esteem, for some reason at the same time makes a group of your comrades laugh. Oh, I was never liked, even in school. I've never been liked anywhere. Even Lukerya cannot like me. The incident in the regiment, though a consequence of this dislike for me, without a doubt bore an accidental character. I mention this because there's nothing more exasperating and intolerable than to be ruined by an incident that might or might not have happened, by an unfortunate chain of circumstances that might have passed over, like a cloud. It's humiliating for an educated man. The incident was as follows.

During the intermission at the theatre I went to the bar. Hussar A—v came in suddenly and began talking loudly with two of his fellow hussars in the presence of all the officers and public gathered there about how Bezumtsev, the captain of our regiment, had just caused a scandal in the corridor 'and he seems to be drunk'. The conversation moved on to other things; besides, there had been a mistake, because Captain Bezumtsev wasn't drunk, and there hadn't really been a scandal. The hussars began talking about something else, and that was the end of it, but the next day the story made its way to our regiment, and at once they began saying how I was the only person at the bar from our regiment and that when Hussar A—v spoke insolently of Captain Bezumtsev I had not gone over to A—v and put a stop to it by reprimanding him. But why on earth should I have done that? If he had it in for Bezumtsev, then it was their personal affair, and why should I get involved? Meanwhile, the officers began to take the position that the affair was not personal but concerned the regiment, and that since I was the only officer of our regiment present, I had proved by my conduct to all the officers at the bar as well as the public that there might be officers in our regiment who were not overly scrupulous concerning their honour and the regiment's. I could not agree with this verdict. I was given to understand that I might still set everything right even now, belatedly, if I should wish to demand a formal explanation from A—v. I did not wish to do so and since I was annoyed, I refused with pride. I then at once resigned my commission – and that's the whole story. I left proud, but with my spirit crushed. My mind and will both foundered. It was just then that my sister's husband squandered our little fortune and my portion of it, a tiny portion, so I was left on the street without a kopeck. I could have found employment in a private business, but I didn't: after wearing my splendid regimental uniform I couldn't go work on some railroad. And so – if it's shame, let it be shame, if it's disgrace, let it be disgrace, if it's degradation, let it be degradation, and the worse, the better – that's what I chose. There followed three years of gloomy memories, even of the Vyazemsky House. A year and a half ago a rich old lady, my godmother, died in Moscow and among other bequests unexpectedly left me 3,000 in her will. I gave it some thought and then decided my fate. I settled on the pawnshop, with no apologies to anyone: money, then a corner and – a new life far away from my former memories – that was the plan. Nevertheless, my gloomy past and the reputation of my honour, forever ruined, tormented me every hour, every minute. But then I married. By chance or not – I don't know. But when I brought her into my house, I thought that I was bringing a friend, I greatly needed a friend. But I saw clearly that my friend had to be prepared, given the finishing touches, and even defeated. And could I have explained anything straight off like that to this sixteen-year-old girl with her prejudices? For example, how could I, without the accidental assistance of the terrible catastrophe with the revolver, have convinced her that I wasn't a coward and that I had been unjustly accused by the regiment of being a coward? But the catastrophe arrived just at the right moment. Having stood up to the revolver, I had avenged all of my gloomy past. And even though nobody knew about it, *she* knew about it, and that was everything for me, because she was everything to me, all my hopes for the future in my dreams! She was the only person whom I was preparing for myself, and I didn't need another – and now she knew everything; at least she knew that she had unjustly hurried to join my enemies. This thought delighted me. In her eyes I could no longer be a scoundrel, but merely a peculiar person, and even this thought, after everything that had happened, did not at all displease me: peculiarity is not a vice; on the contrary, it sometimes attracts the feminine character. In a word, I deliberately postponed the finale: what had taken place was more than sufficient, for the time being, for my peace of mind and contained more than enough pictures and material for my dreams. That's the nasty thing about this – I'm a dreamer: I had enough material; as for her, I thought that *she would wait.*

And so the whole winter passed in some sort of expectation of something. I liked to steal looks at her, when she happened to be sitting at her little table. She would be busy with her needlework, with the linen, and in the evenings she would sometimes read books which she would take from my bookcase. The choice of books in the bookcase should also have spoken in my favour. She hardly ever went out. Every day after dinner, before dusk, I would take her for a walk and we would go for our constitutional, but not completely in silence, as before. I precisely tried to make it look as though we weren't being silent and were speaking harmoniously, but as I've already said we both avoided getting carried away talking. I was doing this on purpose, while she, I thought, needed to be 'given time'. Of course, it's strange that it did not once occur to me until almost the very end of the winter that though I liked to look at her on the sly, I never once caught her looking at me that whole winter! I thought that it was timidity on her part. Moreover, she had an air about her of such timid meekness, such weakness after her illness. No, better to bide one's time and – 'and she will suddenly come to you on her own . . .'

That thought delighted me irresistibly. I will add one thing: sometimes it was as if I had deliberately inflamed myself and really brought my heart and mind to the point that I would feel that I had been wronged by her. And so it continued for some time. But my hatred could never ripen and take root in my soul. And I even felt that it was only some sort of game. And even then, although I had dissolved our marriage by buying the bed and screen, never, never could I see her as a criminal. And not because I judged her crime lightly, but because it made sense to forgive her completely, from the very first day, even before I bought the bed. In a word, this was a strange move on my part, for I am morally stern. On the contrary, in my eyes she was so defeated, so humiliated, so crushed that I sometimes felt tormenting pity for her, even though at the same time I sometimes definitely found the idea of her humiliation pleasing. The idea of our inequality pleased me . . .

That winter it so happened that I deliberately performed several good deeds. I forgave two debts, I gave money to one poor woman without any pledge. And I didn't tell my wife about this, and I hadn't done this so that she would find out; but the woman came to thank me herself, she was practically on her knees. And that was how it became known; it seemed to me that she was truly pleased to find out about the woman.

But spring was approaching, it was already the middle of April, the storm windows had been taken down, and the sun began to light up our silent rooms with its bright pencils of light. But scales hung before my eyes and blinded my reason. Fateful, terrible scales! How did it come about that they suddenly fell from my eyes and that I suddenly could see clearly and understand everything! Was it chance, was it that the appointed day had come, was it a ray of sunshine that had kindled the thought and conjecture in my benumbed mind? No, it wasn't a matter of a thought but rather a nerve began to play up, a nerve that had grown numb began to quiver and came to life and illuminated my entire benumbed soul and my demonic pride. It was as if I had suddenly jumped up from my seat then. And it happened suddenly and unexpectedly. It happened towards evening, at about five o'clock, after dinner . . .

II. THE SCALES SUDDENLY FALL

A couple of words first. A month earlier I had noticed a strange pensiveness in her, not just silence, but pensiveness. I had also noticed this suddenly. She was sitting at her work at the time, her head bent over her sewing, and she didn't see that I was looking at her. And suddenly I was struck by how delicate and thin she had become, that her face was pale, her lips were drained of colour – all this as a whole, taken together with her pensiveness, shocked me all at once in the extreme. I had already heard earlier a little dry cough, particularly at night. I got up at once and set off to ask Schroeder to pay us a visit, without saying anything to her.

Schroeder came the following day. She was very surprised and looked first at Schroeder and then at me.

'But I'm fine,' she said with an uncertain smile.

Schroeder didn't examine her very thoroughly (these medical men sometimes are condescendingly offhand), and merely told me in the other room that it was the remnants of her illness and that come spring it wouldn't be a bad idea to take a trip somewhere to the sea or if that were not possible, then simply to find a place in the country. In a word, he didn't say anything other than that there was some weakness or something of the sort. When Schroeder had gone, she suddenly said to me again, looking at me terribly seriously:

'I'm really, really fine.'

But after saying this, she then and there suddenly flushed, apparently from shame. Apparently, it was shame. Oh, now I understand: She was ashamed that I was still *her husband*, that I was taking care of her as if I were still her real husband. But I didn't understand then and ascribed her blush to humility. (The scales!)

And then, a month later, between five and six o'clock, in April, on a bright sunny day I was sitting in the shop and doing the accounts. Suddenly I heard her in our room, at her table, over her work, singing ever so softly . . . This new development made a tremendous impression on me, and to this day I don't understand it. Until then I had almost never heard her sing, except perhaps in the very first days when I brought her into my house and we could still have some fun, target shooting with the revolver. Then her voice was still rather strong, ringing, though a bit off-key, but terribly pleasant and healthy. But now her little song sounded so feeble – oh, not that it was doleful (it was some romance), but it was as if there was something cracked, broken, in her voice, as if the little voice couldn't cope, as if the song itself were ailing. She was singing under her breath, and suddenly, after rising, the voice broke – such a poor little voice, it broke so pitifully; she cleared her throat and started singing again, ever so softly, you could barely hear her . . .

My agitation may be laughable, but no one will ever understand why I had become so agitated! No, I didn't feel sorry for her yet; it was still something altogether different. At the beginning, for the first moments at least, I suddenly felt bewilderment and terrible surprise, terrible and strange, painful and almost vindictive: 'She is singing and in my presence! *Has she forgotten about me, is that it?*'

Completely shaken, I stayed where I was, then I suddenly rose, took my hat and left, without thinking it through, as it were. At least I didn't know why or where I was going. Lukerya started helping me on with my coat.

'She sings?' I said to Lukerya unintentionally. She didn't understand and looked at me, still not understanding; but I really had been incomprehensible.

'Is this the first time that she's been singing?'

'No, she sometimes sings when you're not here,' Lukerya replied.

I remember everything. I walked down the stairs, went out into the street and set off for nowhere in particular. I walked as far as the corner and began to stare off into the distance. People passed by me, jostled me, but I didn't feel it. I hailed a cab and told him to take me to the Police Bridge, I don't know why. But then I suddenly changed my mind and gave him a twenty-kopeck piece.

'That's for your trouble,' I said, laughing senselessly, but some sort of rapture had suddenly begun to fill my heart.

I turned around and went home, quickening my step. The cracked, poor, broken little note suddenly rang out in my heart again. It took my breath away. The scales were falling, falling from my eyes! If she'd started singing in my presence, then she had forgotten about me – that's what was clear and terrible. My heart sensed this. But rapture shone in my soul and overcame my fear.

Oh, the irony of fate! You see, there had been nothing else and there could not have been anything else in my soul all winter except this very rapture, but where had I myself been all winter long? Had I been there with my soul? I ran up the stairs in a great hurry, I don't know whether I walked in timidly or not. I remember only that the entire floor seemed to be rippling and it was as if I were floating down a river. I walked into the room, she was sitting in the same place, sewing, with her head bent, but no longer singing. She threw me a fleeting and incurious glance, but it wasn't even a glance, merely the usual, indifferent gesture one makes when somebody enters a room.

I walked straight up to her and sat down on a chair right beside her, like a madman. She gave me a quick look, as though she were frightened: I took her by the hand and I don't remember what I said to her, that is, what I wanted to say, because I couldn't even speak properly. My voice kept breaking and wouldn't obey me. And I didn't know what to say, I just kept gasping for breath.

'Let's talk ... you know ... say something!' I suddenly babbled something stupid – oh, but was I capable of making sense? She flinched again and recoiled, badly frightened, looking at my face, but suddenly – *stern surprise* appeared in her eyes. Yes, surprise, and *stern*. She was looking at me wide-eyed. This sternness, this stern surprise came crashing down on me all at once: 'So you still want love? Love?' that surprise seemed to ask suddenly, although she was silent as well. But I could read it all, all of it. My whole being was shaken and I simply fell to the ground at her feet. Yes, I collapsed at her feet. She quickly jumped up, but I restrained her by taking hold of both her hands with extraordinary force.

And I fully understood my despair, oh, I understood! But would you believe it, rapture was seething in my heart so irrepressibly that I thought I would die. I kissed her feet in ecstasy and happiness. Yes, in happiness, immeasurable and infinite, yet understanding nonetheless all my hopeless despair! I wept, said something, but couldn't speak. Her fright and surprise suddenly gave way to some anxious thought, some extreme question, and she looked at me strangely, wildly even – she wanted to understand something quickly, and she smiled. She was terribly ashamed that I was

kissing her feet, and she kept moving back, but I would at
once kiss the spot on the floor where she had been standing.
She saw this and suddenly began to laugh from shame (you
know how people laugh from shame). Hysterics weren't far
off, I saw that, her hands quivered – I didn't give it a thought
and kept muttering that I loved her, that I wouldn't get up,
'. . . let me kiss your dress . . . I'll worship you like this for
as long as you live . . .' I don't know, I don't remember – and
suddenly she burst out into sobs and started trembling; a
terrible fit of hysteria had set in. I had frightened her.

I carried her over to the bed. When the fit had passed, she
sat up on the bed and with a terribly distraught look, seized
me by the hands and pleaded with me to calm myself:
'Enough, don't torment yourself, calm yourself!' and she
began to weep again. I didn't leave her side all that evening.
I kept telling her that I'd take her to Boulogne to bathe in
the sea, now, right away, in two weeks, that she had such a
cracked little voice, I had heard it earlier that day, that I
would close the pawnshop, sell it to Dobronravov, that everything would begin afresh, and the main thing, to Boulogne,
to Boulogne! She listened and was still afraid. She was more
and more afraid. But that wasn't the main thing for me, but
rather that I more and more irrepressibly wanted to lie down
again at her feet, and once again, to kiss, to kiss the ground
on which her feet stood, and to idolize her and – 'I'll ask
nothing more of you, nothing,' I kept repeating every minute. 'Don't answer me anything, don't take any notice of me
at all, and only let me look at you from the corner, turn me
into your thing, into your little dog . . .' She wept.

'*But I thought that you were going to leave me like that,*'

suddenly burst forth from her involuntarily, so involuntarily
that perhaps she didn't notice at all how she had said it, and
yet – oh, it was the most important, her most fateful word
and the most comprehensible for me that evening, and it was
as if it had slashed my heart like a knife. It explained everything to me, everything, but as long as she was there beside
me, before my eyes, I went on hoping irrepressibly and
was terribly happy. Oh, I wore her out terribly that evening
and I understood that, but I kept thinking that I would
change everything at once. Finally, towards nightfall, she
broke down completely; I persuaded her to go to sleep, and
she immediately fell sound asleep. I expected delirium, and
there was delirium, but it was very mild. I got up during the
night every few minutes, and would quietly go in my slippers
to look at her. I wrung my hands over her, as I looked at this
sick being lying on that pathetic little cot, the iron bedstead
that I had bought for her then for three roubles. I got down
on my knees but I didn't dare kiss her feet while she was
sleeping (against her wishes!). I would start praying to God,
and then jump up again. Lukerya watched me closely and
kept coming out of the kitchen. I went to her and told her
to go to bed and that tomorrow 'something quite different'
would begin.

And I believed that blindly, madly, terribly. Oh, I was
surging with rapture, rapture. I couldn't wait for tomorrow.
The main thing, I didn't believe in any misfortune, despite
the symptoms. My powers of understanding had not yet fully
returned, even though the scales had fallen, and for a long,
long time would not return – oh, not until today, not until
this very day! And how, how could my understanding have

returned then: you see, she was still alive then, you see, she was right there before me, and I before her. 'She'll wake up tomorrow, and I'll tell her all this, and she'll see it all.' That was my reasoning then, clear and simple, hence the rapture! The main thing was this trip to Boulogne. For some reason I thought that Boulogne was everything, that there was something final about Boulogne. 'To Boulogne, to Boulogne! . . .' I waited for morning in a state of madness.

III. I UNDERSTAND ALL TOO WELL

But this was only a few days ago, you see, five days, only five days ago, just last Tuesday! No, no, if only there had been a little more time, if only she had waited just a little bit longer and – and I would have dispelled the darkness! And hadn't she calmed down? The very next day she listened to me with a smile even, despite her confusion. The main thing was that during all this time, all five days, she was either confused or ashamed . . . She was also afraid, very afraid. I don't dispute it, I won't deny it, like some madman: there was fear, but then how could she not be afraid? You see, we'd been strangers to each other for so long, we had grown so far apart from one another, and suddenly all this . . . But I didn't pay attention to her fear – something new was shining! . . . Yes, it's undoubtedly true that I'd made a mistake. And perhaps even many mistakes. And as soon as we woke up the next day, when it was still morning (this was on Wednesday), I suddenly made a mistake right away: I suddenly made her my friend. I was in a hurry, much too much of a hurry, but a confession was necessary, essential – and much more than a confession! I didn't even conceal that which I had concealed from myself all my life. I told her straight out that I had done nothing all winter long but be certain of her love. I explained to her that the pawnshop had been merely the degradation of my will and mind, my personal idea of self-flagellation and self-exaltation. I explained to her that I had indeed turned coward that time at the bar, and that it was owing to my character, my touchiness: I was struck by the surroundings, I was struck by the bar; I was struck by how I would end up looking in all this and wouldn't it end up looking stupid? I didn't turn coward on account of the duel, but because it would end up looking stupid . . . And then later I didn't want to admit it, and tormented everyone, and tormented her for it as well, and then I married her so that I could torment her on account of it. In general, for the most part I spoke as though I were in a fever. She herself took me by the hands and begged me to stop: 'You're exaggerating . . . you're tormenting yourself', and the tears would begin again, and again there'd almost be a fit of hysteria. She kept pleading with me not to say or remember any of this.

I paid little or no attention to her pleas: spring, Boulogne! There was the sun, there was our new sun, that was all I talked about! I locked up the shop, handed over the business to Dobronravov. I suddenly suggested to her that we give away everything to the poor, except for the initial 3,000 I had received from my godmother, which we would use to travel to Boulogne, and then we'd come back and begin our new working life. And so it was decided, because she didn't say anything . . . she merely smiled. And I believe she smiled more out of a sense of delicacy, so as not to upset me. Of course, I saw that I was a burden to her, don't think that I was so stupid or such an egoist that I didn't see that. I saw everything, everything, right down to the last detail, I saw and knew better than anyone else; my despair was there for all to see!

I told her everything about myself and about her. And about Lukerya. I told her that I had wept . . . Oh, I'd change the subject, you see, I was also trying not to remind her of certain things at all. And, you see, she even livened up once or twice, you see, I remember, I remember! Why do you say that I looked and saw nothing? And if only *this* had not happened, everything would have been resurrected. You see, it was she who told me the day before yesterday, when the conversation turned to reading and what she had read that winter – you see, it was she who told me and laughed, when she recalled that scene between Gil Blas and the Archbishop of Granada. And what a childish laugh, sweet, just like when she was still my fiancée (an instant! an instant!); I was so happy! I was terribly struck, however, by the archbishop: you see, that meant she had found enough peace of mind and happiness to laugh at that masterpiece while she sat there that winter. That means that she had already begun to find herself wholly at peace, that she had already begun to be wholly persuaded that I would leave her *like that*. 'I thought that you were going to leave me *like that*' – that's what she had said then on Tuesday! Oh, the thought of a ten-year-old girl! And you see, she believed, believed that everything would in fact remain *like that*: she at her table, I at mine, and that's how it would be for both of us until we were sixty. And suddenly – here I come forward, her husband, and her husband needs love! Oh, the incomprehensibility, oh, my blindness!

It was also a mistake to look at her with rapture; I should have exercised restraint, because the rapture frightened her. But you see, I did exercise restraint, I didn't kiss her feet anymore. Not once did I make a show of the fact . . . well, that I was her husband – oh, and it didn't even cross my mind, I only worshipped her! But you see, I couldn't be completely silent, I couldn't say nothing at all, you see! I suddenly told her that I enjoyed her conversation and that I considered her incomparably, incomparably more educated and developed than I. Embarrassed, she blushed bright red and said that I was exaggerating. At this point, unable to contain myself, I foolishly told her what rapture I'd felt when I stood behind the door and listened to her duel, a duel of innocence with that beast, and how I had taken pleasure in her intelligence, her sparkling wit, combined with such childlike simple-heartedness. She seemed to shudder all over, murmured again that I was exaggerating, but suddenly her whole face darkened, she covered it with her hands and burst into sobs . . . Here I was unable to hold myself back: I again fell down before her, I again started to kiss her feet and again it ended in a fit, just as it had on Tuesday. That was yesterday evening, but the next morning . . .

Next morning?! Madman, but that morning was today, just now, only just now!

Listen and consider carefully: you see, when we met just

now (this was after yesterday's attack), she even struck me with her calmness, that's how it was! While all night long I had been trembling with fear over what had happened yesterday. But suddenly she comes up to me, stands before me and with her arms folded (just now, just now!), began by telling me that she's a criminal, that she knows this, that the crime has tormented her all winter long, and is tormenting her now ... that she values my magnanimity all too much ... 'I'll be your true wife, I'll respect you ...' Here I jumped up and embraced her like a madman! I kissed her, I kissed her face, her lips, like a husband, for the first time after a long separation. But why did I go out just now, for only two hours ... our foreign passports ... Oh, God! If only I had returned five minutes earlier, just five minutes! ... And now there's this crowd at our gate, these eyes fixed on me ... Oh, Lord!

Lukerya says (oh, I won't let Lukerya go now for anything, she knows everything, she was here all winter, she'll tell me everything), she says that after I left the house and only some twenty minutes before my return – she suddenly went into our room to see the mistress to ask her something, I don't remember what, and she saw that her icon (the same icon of the Mother of God) had been taken down and was on the table before her, and that her mistress seemed to have been praying before it. 'What's wrong, mistress?' 'Nothing, Lukerya, you may go ... Wait, Lukerya,' she walked up to her and kissed her. 'Are you happy, mistress?' I ask. 'Yes, Lukerya.' 'The master should have come to ask your forgiveness long ago ... Thank God, you've made up.' 'All right, Lukerya,' she says, 'leave me, Lukerya.' And she smiled, but so strangely. So strangely that ten minutes later Lukerya suddenly went back to look in on her: 'She was standing by the wall, right by the window, she had placed her hand on the wall, and laid her head on her hand, she was standing like that and thinking. And she was so lost in thought standing there that she didn't hear me standing there and watching her from the other room. I saw that she was smiling, as it were, standing, thinking and smiling. I looked at her, turned around ever so quietly and walked out, thinking to myself, only suddenly I hear the window being opened. I at once went to say that "it's fresh, mistress, you'll catch cold" – and suddenly I see that she's climbed up on to the window and is already standing there upright, in the open window, with her back towards me and holding the icon. My heart just sank then and I cried out: "Mistress, mistress!" She heard, made a move as if to turn around towards me, but didn't, instead she took a step, clutched the icon to her breast – and threw herself out the window!'

I only remember that when I entered the gates she was still warm. The main thing is that they're all looking at me. At first they were shouting, but then they suddenly fell silent and they all make way for me and . . . and she's lying there with the icon. I remember, though darkly, that I walked over in silence and looked for a long time, and they all gathered round and are saying something to me. Lukerya was there, but I didn't see her. She says that she spoke with me. I remember only that tradesman: he kept shouting at me 'only a handful of blood came out of her mouth, a handful, a handful!' and pointing to the blood on a stone. I think I touched the blood with my finger, smeared some on my finger, looked at my finger (I remember that), and he kept saying to me: 'A handful, a handful!'

'And what do you mean "a handful"?' I wailed, they say, with all my might, I raised my arms and threw myself at him ...

Oh, it's absurd, absurd! Incomprehensibility! Improbability! Impossibility!

IV. ONLY FIVE MINUTES TOO LATE

But is it really? Is it really probable? Can one really say that it was possible? Why, for what reason did this woman die?

Oh, believe me, I understand; but why she died is still a question. She was frightened of my love, she asked herself seriously whether she should accept it or not, and she couldn't bear the question and it was better to die. I know, I know, there's no use in racking my brains over it: she had made too many promises, got frightened that she couldn't keep them – that's clear. There are a number of circumstances here that are quite terrible.

Because why did she die? The question persists, all the same. The question hammers, hammers away in my brain. I would even have left her *like that* if she had wished to be left *like that*. She didn't believe it, that's what! No, no, I'm lying, that's not it at all. It was simply because with me it had to be honest: to love meant to love completely, and not like she would have loved the merchant. And since she was too chaste, too pure to agree to a love like a merchant needs, she didn't want to deceive me. She didn't want to deceive me with half a love or a quarter of a love under the guise of love. She was much too honest, that's what it is, gentlemen! I wanted to cultivate breadth of heart then, do you remember? A strange thought.

I'm terribly curious: did she respect me? I don't know. Did she despise me or not? I don't think she did. It's terribly strange: why didn't it occur to me all winter long that she despised me? I was utterly convinced of the contrary right until the moment when she looked at me then with *stern surprise*. Precisely, *stern*. It was then that I understood at once that she despised me. I understood irrevocably and forever! Ah, let her, let her despise me, for her whole life even, but let her live, live! Just now she was still walking, talking. I don't at all understand how she could throw herself out the window! And how could I have supposed that even five minutes earlier? I summoned Lukerya. I won't let Lukerya go now for anything, not for anything!

Oh, we could still have come to an understanding. It's just that we had grown so terribly unused to each other during the winter, but couldn't we have become accustomed to one another again? Why, why couldn't we have come together and begun a new life again? I'm magnanimous, and so is she – that's the point of connection! Just a few words more, two days, no more, and she would have understood everything.

The main thing, it's a pity that it all comes down to chance – simple, barbaric inertia, chance. That's the pity of it! All of five minutes, I was only five minutes late! If I had arrived five minutes earlier – the moment would have passed by, like a cloud, and it would never have occurred to her again. And it would have ended by her understanding everything. But now the rooms stand empty again and I'm alone once again. There's the pendulum ticking, it doesn't care, it doesn't feel sorry for anyone. There's no one – that's the awful thing!

I pace, I keep pacing. I know, I know, don't try to put words in my mouth: you think it's ridiculous that I complain about chance and the five minutes? But it's obvious, you see. Consider one thing: she didn't even leave a note saying, 'Don't blame anyone for my death', like everyone does. Could she really not have considered that even Lukerya might get into trouble? They might say, 'You were alone with her, so you must have pushed her.' In any event, she would have been dragged away, innocent though she was, if four people in the courtyard hadn't seen from the windows of the wing and the courtyard how she stood there holding the icon and hurled herself down. But, you see, that's chance as well that people were standing and saw it. No, this was all a moment, just one inexplicable moment. Suddenness and fantasy! So what if she was praying before the icon? That doesn't mean that this was before death. The entire moment lasted, perhaps, all of some ten minutes, the entire decision – precisely when she was standing by the wall, with her head resting on her arm, and smiling. The thought flew into her head, her head started spinning and – and she couldn't withstand it.

It was a clear misunderstanding, say what you will. She could still have lived with me. But what if it was anaemia? Simply on account of anaemia, the exhaustion of vital energy? She had grown tired during the winter, that's what it was . . .

I was late!!!

How very thin she is in the coffin, how sharp her little nose has become! Her eyelashes lie like arrows. And she fell, you see – without smashing or breaking anything! Just this one 'handful of blood'. A dessertspoon, that is. Internal concussion. A strange thought: What if it were possible not to bury her? Because if they take her away, then ... Oh, no, it's almost impossible that she'll be taken away! Oh, of course, I know that she must be taken away, I'm not a madman and I'm not the least bit delirious; on the contrary, my mind has never been so lucid – but how can it be that again there'll be no one in the house, again the two rooms, and again I'm alone with the pledges. Delirium, delirium, that's where the delirium lies! I tormented her – that's what it was!

What are your laws to me now? What do I need with your customs, your ways, your life, your government, your faith? Let your judges judge me, let them take me to court, to your public court, and I will say that I acknowledge nothing. The judge will shout: 'Silence, officer!' And I will cry out to him: 'What power do you now possess that I should obey you? Why has dark inertia shattered that which was dearest of all? What need have I now of your laws? I part company with you.' Oh, it's all the same to me!

Blind, she's blind! Dead, she doesn't hear! You don't know with what paradise I would have surrounded you. The paradise was in my soul; I would have planted it all round you! Well, you wouldn't have loved me – so be it, what of it? Everything would have been *like that*, everything would have stayed *like that*. You would have talked to me only as a friend – and we would have rejoiced and laughed with joy, as we looked into each other's eyes. That's how we would have lived. And if you had fallen in love with somebody else – well, so be it, so be it! You would have walked with him and laughed, while I looked on from the other side of the street ... Oh, let it be anything, anything, if only she would open her eyes just once! For one moment, just one! If she would look at me as she did just now, when she stood before me and swore to be my faithful wife! Oh, she would have understood it all in one glance!

Inertia! Oh, nature! People are alone on this earth – that's the problem! 'Is there a man alive on the field?' the Russian *bogatyr* cries out. And I cry out as well, though I am not a *bogatyr*, and no one answers. They say that the sun gives life to the universe. The sun will rise and – look at it, isn't it dead? Everything is dead, the dead are everywhere. There are only people, and all around them is silence – that's the earth. 'People, love one another' – who said that? Whose commandment is that? The pendulum ticks insensibly, disgustingly. It's two o'clock in the morning. Her little shoes are by the bed, as if they were waiting for her ... No, seriously, when they take her away tomorrow, what will become of me?

1876

1. BOCCACCIO · *Mrs Rosie and the Priest*
2. GERARD MANLEY HOPKINS · *As kingfishers catch fire*
3. *The Saga of Gunnlaug Serpent-tongue*
4. THOMAS DE QUINCEY · *On Murder Considered as One of the Fine Arts*
5. FRIEDRICH NIETZSCHE · *Aphorisms on Love and Hate*
6. JOHN RUSKIN · *Traffic*
7. PU SONGLING · *Wailing Ghosts*
8. JONATHAN SWIFT · *A Modest Proposal*
9. *Three Tang Dynasty Poets*
10. WALT WHITMAN · *On the Beach at Night Alone*
11. KENKŌ · *A Cup of Sake Beneath the Cherry Trees*
12. BALTASAR GRACIÁN · *How to Use Your Enemies*
13. JOHN KEATS · *The Eve of St Agnes*
14. THOMAS HARDY · *Woman much missed*
15. GUY DE MAUPASSANT · *Femme Fatale*
16. MARCO POLO · *Travels in the Land of Serpents and Pearls*
17. SUETONIUS · *Caligula*
18. APOLLONIUS OF RHODES · *Jason and Medea*
19. ROBERT LOUIS STEVENSON · *Olalla*
20. KARL MARX AND FRIEDRICH ENGELS · *The Communist Manifesto*
21. PETRONIUS · *Trimalchio's Feast*
22. JOHANN PETER HEBEL · *How a Ghastly Story Was Brought to Light by a Common or Garden Butcher's Dog*
23. HANS CHRISTIAN ANDERSEN · *The Tinder Box*
24. RUDYARD KIPLING · *The Gate of the Hundred Sorrows*
25. DANTE · *Circles of Hell*
26. HENRY MAYHEW · *Of Street Piemen*
27. HAFEZ · *The nightingales are drunk*
28. GEOFFREY CHAUCER · *The Wife of Bath*
29. MICHEL DE MONTAIGNE · *How We Weep and Laugh at the Same Thing*
30. THOMAS NASHE · *The Terrors of the Night*
31. EDGAR ALLAN POE · *The Tell-Tale Heart*
32. MARY KINGSLEY · *A Hippo Banquet*
33. JANE AUSTEN · *The Beautifull Cassandra*
34. ANTON CHEKHOV · *Gooseberries*
35. SAMUEL TAYLOR COLERIDGE · *Well, they are gone, and here must I remain*
36. JOHANN WOLFGANG VON GOETHE · *Sketchy, Doubtful, Incomplete Jottings*
37. CHARLES DICKENS · *The Great Winglebury Duel*
38. HERMAN MELVILLE · *The Maldive Shark*
39. ELIZABETH GASKELL · *The Old Nurse's Story*
40. NIKOLAY LESKOV · *The Steel Flea*

41. HONORÉ DE BALZAC · *The Atheist's Mass*
42. CHARLOTTE PERKINS GILMAN · *The Yellow Wall-Paper*
43. C.P. CAVAFY · *Remember, Body . . .*
44. FYODOR DOSTOEVSKY · *The Meek One*
45. GUSTAVE FLAUBERT · *A Simple Heart*
46. NIKOLAI GOGOL · *The Nose*
47. SAMUEL PEPYS · *The Great Fire of London*
48. EDITH WHARTON · *The Reckoning*
49. HENRY JAMES · *The Figure in the Carpet*
50. WILFRED OWEN · *Anthem For Doomed Youth*
51. WOLFGANG AMADEUS MOZART · *My Dearest Father*
52. PLATO · *Socrates' Defence*
53. CHRISTINA ROSSETTI · *Goblin Market*
54. *Sindbad the Sailor*
55. SOPHOCLES · *Antigone*
56. RYŪNOSUKE AKUTAGAWA · *The Life of a Stupid Man*
57. LEO TOLSTOY · *How Much Land Does A Man Need?*
58. GIORGIO VASARI · *Leonardo da Vinci*
59. OSCAR WILDE · *Lord Arthur Savile's Crime*
60. SHEN FU · *The Old Man of the Moon*
61. AESOP · *The Dolphins, the Whales and the Gudgeon*
62. MATSUO BASHŌ · *Lips too Chilled*
63. EMILY BRONTË · *The Night is Darkening Round Me*
64. JOSEPH CONRAD · *To-morrow*
65. RICHARD HAKLUYT · *The Voyage of Sir Francis Drake Around the Whole Globe*
66. KATE CHOPIN · *A Pair of Silk Stockings*
67. CHARLES DARWIN · *It was snowing butterflies*
68. BROTHERS GRIMM · *The Robber Bridegroom*
69. CATULLUS · *I Hate and I Love*
70. HOMER · *Circe and the Cyclops*
71. D. H. LAWRENCE · *Il Duro*
72. KATHERINE MANSFIELD · *Miss Brill*
73. OVID · *The Fall of Icarus*
74. SAPPHO · *Come Close*
75. IVAN TURGENEV · *Kasyan from the Beautiful Lands*
76. VIRGIL · *O Cruel Alexis*
77. H. G. WELLS · *A Slip under the Microscope*
78. HERODOTUS · *The Madness of Cambyses*
79. *Speaking of Siva*
80. *The Dhammapada*